SHADOWS
OF PARIS

SHADOWS OF PARIS

ERIC D. LEHMAN

HOMEBOUND
PUBLICATIONS
WWW.HOMEBOUNDPUBLICATIONS.COM

HOMEBOUND PUBLICATIONS

Ensuring the mainstream isn't the only stream.

Copyright © 2016 by Eric D. Lehman
All Rights Reserved
Printed in the United States of America
as well as the United Kingdom and Australia.

First Edition Trade Paperback

Paperback ISBN 978-1-938846-92-2
Front Cover Image © IM_Photo | Shutterstock.com
Cover and Interior Designed by Leslie M. Browning

www.homeboundpublications.com

10 9 8 7 6 5 4 3 2 1

Homebound Publications greatly values the natural environment and
invests in environmental conservation. Our books are printed on paper
with chain of custody certification from the Forest Stewardship Council,
Sustainable Forestry Initiative, and the Program for the Endorsement
of Forest Certification. In addition, each year Homebound Publications
donates 1% of our net profit to a humanitarian or ecological charity.

ALTHOUGH I HAVE NEVER BEEN A RELIGIOUS MAN, I began to walk to Notre Dame after class every day that December. I took a seat somewhere in the vast transept and put all thoughts of the little monsters I taught out of my head. There were other places I could have gone: the national library, the cafes frequented by famous writers, or the dozens of nearby museums. But somehow my lack of religious spirit made Notre Dame a refuge from thought, which is what I wanted, I suppose.

1

As I approached from the Pont St. Louis, naked winter trees framed the flying buttresses like the fingers of underground giants. I often felt like one of the ancient Celts who settled the Ile de Cite millennia before, coming to a place beyond my own scope or imagination, completely baffled by both the artistry of its creation and the fervor behind it. I avoided the small park along the Seine that faced the Latin Quarter, which still unaccountably had purple pansies, even in the snapping wind. Inside, I would find a chair next to one of the stone pillars and lean on it, the vaulted roof and endless stained glass above me both austere and ornate. The murmur of the tourists and the piped-in plainsong always lulled me into reverie without memory, without any sense of my own future or past.

Besides, it was close to the small private school in the Marais where I taught English, and I could walk to it quite readily at the end of a grueling day of verb conjugation. I had come to Paris a few months earlier, but not for the same reasons those dead writers came. The École Eustache near Les Halles had an opening, and I had taken it, out of desperation. That is, I was not desperate for a job, but for a convenient excuse.

Four weeks into this daily vigil I sat and studied the iron chandeliers and the carved wooden pulpits, all decorated for a Christmas that had just passed me by. I had spent it in my small apartment on Rue Tiquetonne, cooking my usual meal of rice and English tea. I reread *Jane Eyre*, which I was teaching in the spring, when I would advance from grammar to my supposed specialty, British Literature. It had not been my specialty in graduate school, and it is not now, these many years later. But this is no surprise. I was a different person back then.

There's not much in saying that; I have been at least four or five people so far, and I'm sure I have a couple left. We are many people, students and teachers, sinners and saints. But sitting there on the day after Christmas in the Cathedral of Notre Dame, I was sure I did not belong on those picture windows.

*   *   *   *

I HAD SEEN MONSIEUR CYGNE IN THE HALLS of the École several times during the autumn semester, but we had never spoken. This was not unusual; I spoke abysmal French and had avoided everyone. When I stopped by the faculty offices to pick up some student folders on

December 27, the large, red-cheeked ogre finally waylaid me in the lunchroom.

"Bonjour, Monsieur Byrnes. Comment allez-vous?"

"Bien, Monsieur…"

"Cygne." He switched to English. "I am the literature teacher here, and so you are technically…my employee?" The man held up a second wine glass and a bottle of Bordeaux. "Join me for a drink."

"Mais non. It's a little early." I glanced at the clock nervously.

"Nonsense! Come here and begin your day correctly." The man paused, tugging a red earlobe. "That is an order?"

"Oui, merci." I said, groaning. I had avoided this so far, because I had no wish to become entangled in office politics or join the senior faculty in their Friday night carousing. In October, the young Mathematics teacher, fresh from the Sorbonne, had made overtures which I had politely refused. In revenge I suspected she had spread word among the students that I was impotent. All this despite the platinum band on my left ring finger.

"So, Monsieur Byrnes. How is it you come to us in Paris with such bad French?" He laughed and clinked his small glass against mine. "I do not say this to be rude, of course. I am merely…curious?"

I tried to laugh and took a sniff of the smooth, black-berry nose of the wine. It had been a long time since I had anything but tea. "Well, Monsieur Cygne, I have to apologize for that error. I had no intention of coming to France until this July, when I answered the École's ad in the *New York Times*."

"And so you come to us despite having no French? You are very brave, Monsieur!" Cygne drained his glass and poured another. "The students here are, as you know, très mal."

I hesitated. "They are no worse than American students."

"Nonsense! These are the worst students in the entire world. I would stake my life on that." Cygne turned and rummaged in the small refrigerator, pulling out a jar of black olives.

I nodded agreeably, feeling the warm flush of wine hit me. "They are not easy to control with my bad French."

"Oui, oui…" Cygne seemed to fall into a stupor, popping olives into his mouth one by one and spitting the seeds into a metal trash bin.

I filled the space. "Do I have you to thank for the liter-ature class in the spring?"

Cygne slapped a meaty hand on the table. "Yes! A man cannot only teach grammar. It is like living on water with no wine."

I avoided this pitfall. "It will be nice to return to my field."

"Ah, so you, an American, dedicate yourself to British Literature. This is a mystery?"

I wasn't sure if this was an actual question, given Cygne's obvious habit of ending sentences with an inflection, but I answered anyway. "In college, uhm, university, I did study American Literature. But later it was not so appealing to me."

"Hmm…" Cygne looked at me, but did not follow up his question, perhaps finding the subject boring. "And French literature? In translation of course." He puffed a laugh.

"Well, in graduate school I read Sartre, Camus…"

"Bah! That is not literature, that is philosophy. What of Balzac, Zola, Hugo?"

"*The Hunchback*…" I said weakly.

Cygne moved his huge head back and forth, as if shaking off water. "Mais non! I will give you…as your superior…an assignment?"

I smiled uncertainly, hiding my face with my glass.

"Yes, you must read something of the great ones." He pulled a pad of the school's letterhead from his black doctor's bag and scribbled on it. "This is the address of a bookstore. An English bookstore, of course. We do not want to test your French skills. This bookstore, however, specializes in translations from the Spanish, the Russian, et cetera. And of course the French literature is of primary importance there."

"Okay." I took the paper.

"Okay? Yes, okay!" Cygne seemed to find great pleasure in the word. "Okay," he stressed, "because there you will find the keys to Paris, the keys to literature, the keys to life!" He laughed warmly at his own exaggeration.

*   *   *   *

My head swam with the Bordeaux as I walked down the Avenue Saint Denis, ignoring the tabacs and pharmacies. Forget those stupid keys! My own apartment key seemed broken, and only after many minutes and much swearing was I able to force my way inside. I collapsed on the small couch and stared at the exposed wooden beams, cursing Gallic joie de vivre and my own indulgence.

The apartment provided me by the École had previously been occupied for a long time by a Nigerian teacher, and he had left a collection of West African masks, prints, and decorative weapons. Handmade red curtains with intricate gold patterns hung down full-length windows, which would open in the summer to allow smokers and suicides easy access to the open air five stories above the cobbled street. Only two things ruined this cohesive interior. The first was a photo print of Louis Armstrong holding a cigarette and laughing uproariously. In October I had put it in the corner on the floor and turned it around, but the empty space still held the image in my mind. The other was an enormous African pot hunched between the windows, holding a gigantic sheaf of paper leaves, mimicking a vase, I assumed. It was hideous, and completely ruined the otherwise fascinating décor, which I liked for the same reason I liked Notre Dame, because I had no connection with it.

Other than the unique furnishings, the apartment was dreadful, with inconsistent heating, tepid water, and terrible drafts. The bedroom was only slightly larger than the bed, and sloped into one corner, leaving me feeling like I was falling out of bed, even when I huddled on the far side. The kitchen was the size of a small closet, though for my purposes it was more than sufficient. My box of cheap tea bags, jar of oatmeal, and ten pound bag of rice fit snugly on the small shelf, and I used and reused the same pot, mug, and spoon, washing them immediately after use, and letting them dry on the thin wire rack.

The built-in bookshelf in the main was filled with books, all *en francais*. I snorted, thinking back to my conversation with Cygne. Of course I should have learned French properly before presuming to teach in Paris. But they had given me the job knowing full well my weakness in that area. Three years of high school French fifteen years earlier, and a month-long immersion course were not enough. So be it, I thought crossly. What did I need with more French Literature? Sartre and Camus and their ilk had certainly not helped me in my early twenties and in fact...

I stopped that line of thought and rose to make my daily pot of rice. The days before winter session began on January 4th would be endless. I had already planned my classes, and couldn't spend ten hours a day in Notre Dame. I might as well try this bookstore. Cygne could go to hell, but I was not going to let him have the satisfaction of knowing I was a complete failure.

*   *   *   *

THE MAP OF PARIS PROVIDED BY THE ÉCOLE was spotty at best, and it took me nearly an hour to find the little cross-street and square at the eastern end of the Marais. The place was not large, with only a few sycamores, and no fountain. But on the opposite corner, where the old pre-Haussmann rue continued toward another broad avenue, the shop was framed by a black facade with simple red lettering: *Librarie Anglais Rose*. I hesitated, looking the sheet of letterhead. Cygne had written "*Belly of Paris* by Emile Zola. Commence!" next to the address. I knew a little about Zola, primarily his heroic involvement in the Dreyfus affair. It seemed a strange choice for Cygne to make. Why not a classic like Zola's more famous *Germinal* or Hugo's *Les Miserables*? These were books I'd always meant to read, or at least that's what I told myself.

I pushed open the front door and immediately the smell of books drowned me. Stepping in from the cold winter street, the sense of thick, warm closeness was overwhelming. A combination of musty old pages and crisply pressed bindings swirled into my nostrils and made me cough. I reached a steadying hand to the front counter by the register, then jerked it back as something moved there. It was only a black tabby, which stared at me with yellow eyes, and then leapt to the floor, looking back as if beckoning me to follow.

I did, my black wool coat brushing the shelves on each side. At first there seemed to be no particular organization, with new paperbacks shelved next to ancient hardbound tomes. But as I moved I could see that at least the store was arranged by original language. I looked around for a French section, but couldn't find one. With no one at the counter, the entire place seemed empty. I made two cycles around the cramped shelves, nearly tripping over another cat, a blue Persian that contemplated my boots with a sleepy nonchalance. Where had the other cat gone? Was there a secret passage? Finally, behind a wall of stacked books I found an opening leading down.

Step by step I creaked down what I was sure was the oldest staircase in France, steadying myself on shelves of books by Moliere and Montaigne. Aha, the French "M" section! At the bottom of this dangerous chute, I saw the black cat, curling up on a thin table under a lamp. I reached out a hand to pet it, and almost knocked over the lamp when I realized a person was standing directly to my left.

"Bonjour, Monsieur!" A cheery voice rang in my ear.

Recovering my balance, I turned to see a woman step into the arc of the lamplight. She was about a head shorter than me, had mouse-brown hair, and wore a black dress that even to my fashion-ignorant eyes seemed a throwback to the last century. "Oh, bonjour. Emile Zola, s'il vous plaît?" I stammered.

She looked at me with gray eyes that seemed to penetrate my head. Later I would think they were the color of the Seine after rain, or the winter sycamores of the Champ-de-Mars from a distance. They were the sort of eyes that a Greek goddess would have when she was masquerading as a librarian.

"You are American?" She asked in a clear New England accent.

"Yes, I'm sorry. My French is very bad."

"Mine was for the first year I spent in Paris, and now it is only acceptable, or at least that is what my husband tells me."

"Oh…" I said, brilliantly.

"You are here on holiday?" She turned and began shelving books while still looking in my direction.

"No," I said, watching her pale hands unconcernedly shove books into thin cracks. "I teach at the École Eustache near Les Halles."

"English, I assume?"

"No...I'm from Philadelphia," I said.

She laughed, something between a chuckle and a snort. "No, you *teach* English."

"Oh, right. Yes." I stood there like a fool. Then, inspiration struck. "My name is William, William Byrnes."

"I'm Lucy, Lucy Navarre." She imitated my inflection, chuckling away. I suddenly felt comfortable with this underground shade. She continued, "I mean, I'm a Doubleday from Massachusetts, but my husband's last name is Navarre. It's the reason I married him." She considered. "That, and this fabulous store."

"Aha." I said, and tried to regain a little ground. "So, you put that in your vows?"

Again, the laugh, though this time it seemed a little forced. Maybe I had gone too far. "Anyway, I was sent here by a Monsieur Cygne, also from the École . He said you specialize in translations to English."

"Yes, indeed we do, though I am afraid I don't remember your Monsieur Cygne. As you can see, we have so many customers." She waved a hand, which I noticed was ringless.

I laughed now, for the first time in what must have been many years. When I recovered, I saw her iron eyes focused intently on me. "Sorry...I...well, maybe I can change that this coming semester."

"For now perhaps I can help you find something else. What was it? Zola?"

"Oui," I said, then felt like a fool again. "Sorry, habit now..."

"See," she said brightly, "You are already becoming French, like me."

Whatever she was, it was not French, I thought, but said, "That is why I'm here, really. My French literature is quite poor."

"You really are a poisson out of water, Monsieur Byrnes."

"William," I said, and instantly regretted it. "If you don't mind."

"It will be a relief not to stand on ceremony." She moved and I followed her oaky hair down an aisle almost too narrow for my shoulders. It's a good thing I am so thin, I thought, and then nearly stumbled into the woman around the corner, where she was bending over, peering at a low shelf.

"What book was it?"

"*The Belly of Paris?*" I asked, expressing my disbelief at the odd name.

"Oh, of course! You are near Les Halles? That is the belly, or rather it was until the early seventies." She handed me a hardback volume. "But surely that can't be your only purchase today. If your French literature is as bad as you say." The woman, Lucy I reminded myself, briskly moved through the shelves. "This, and this, and this." She began to create a small stack in the crook of her left arm. "And this." She stopped, seeing my horrified face. "Well, perhaps we'd better leave a few for your next visit."

My next visit? I tried not to read too much into that. She was another man's wife, for Keats' sake. And I was wearing a ring… I took the stack. "This will hold me, at least until the New Year."

Lucy laughed, hopping up the squeaking stairs. I took a moment to pet the black cat, and glanced back into the cellar flooded with literature, considering why someone had thought the musty labyrinth an incentive to marriage. There were worse reasons, I supposed.

As I walked back along the endless Rue de Rivoli, I caught my reflection in a shop window. I was smiling broadly, and, shocked, I sat down on a bench by the Hotel De Ville, attacked by waves of nausea. I had no right to be smiling. Absolutely no right at all.

*   *   *   *

I REMAINED IN A MEDITATIVE GLOOM for three days, wondering about the fate of the African teacher who had abandoned all his relics. On New Year's Eve I decided I should begin the Zola book, in case Cygne asked me about it when classes started. After my usual breakfast of oatmeal and strong tea, I arranged myself on the small couch, dangling long legs over the edge. As I entered the world of nineteenth-century Paris along with the exhausted Florent, I found familiar streets and landmarks. The old Les Halles seemed a decadent and strange place for the escaped prisoner from Devil's Island, and completely alien to me. As I read page after page describing the bright vegetables and fresh fish, my frugal regime began to seem even more frugal. The salted meats of the Quenu butcher shop began to make my mouth water and my stomach ache. Rich butter, sizzling fat, crisp leaves of cabbages...the book went on and on. At three in the afternoon I tried to stifle the problem with a heaping bowl of rice, which I salted heavily. An hour later I was starving again. I cursed Cygne for recommending the book, for the torture I was now enduring. Finally, my boots rumbled out the door as the sun was going down.

Boulangeries and bucheries appeared at every step. The Rue Montorgueil still had a flavor of the former Les Halles, and it was swarmed with people shopping for their New Year's Day meals. A rotisserie at one shop spun several chickens dripping with juices; my wallet was out, and a capon in a bag before I knew what I was doing. I bought a loaf of peasant bread, a peppered sausage, and *fromage de montagne*. Returning to the apartment, the smells weakened my knees, and I barely made it up the five flights of stairs. Spreading the feast out on the coffee table, I began to gorge myself, taste buds exploding with savory goodness I hadn't known for years. Finishing the entire chicken and half the loaf of bread, I continued reading in the slanted bed, falling fast asleep long before the New Year.

A police siren woke me a few hours later, and I ran to the bathroom and vomited everything. Afterward, I collapsed back into bed, lying awake listening to the revelers in the streets below. Sirens continued to howl every few minutes, preventing sleep. My tortured mind turned over and over, remorseful and confused. The next morning, though, I had a small piece of cheese with my oatmeal.

*   *   *   *

THE NEW SESSION BEGAN with the usual pranks from the students. I shrugged them off and told them that the top five students who scored on the "examination de William Shakespeare" would have a special prize. They seemed unimpressed and I launched weakly into *A Winter's Tale*. I was more interested in reading Rimbaud and Baudelaire, who echoed the rebellious philosophies of my youth. It was an uncomfortable look in the mirror, but I was hooked nevertheless. Maybe the fact that a lovely bookstore maven had pressed them on me was helping me through. Or perhaps it was only an extension of my guilt to torture myself. Of course, I can look back and say that now, but at the time I think I was unaware of anything but my own misery and its impossible antithesis.

The first week dragged, with only a few scattered words with Monsieur Cygne to break it up.

"So…you like the *Belly*, Monsieur Byrnes?"

"J'ai faim," I said.

He burst into a huge Gallic laugh, slapping my thin shoulder. "Oui! Now you will eat some foie gras with me after class one day?"

"Oui," I groaned.

The examination on *A Winter's Tale* was on Monday, and only three of the students passed. I picked two others that had been well-behaved in my grammar class, and on Wednesday afternoon two teenage girls, three boys, and I tramped into the city together. I had told them to bring a little money, since I was not worried that any would be poor. The students at the École Eustache came from rich families who had squirreled them away like gold heirlooms not meant to be worn.

"Where are we?" asked the more precocious of the two girls.

I assumed she was asking where we were going, but didn't bother to correct her. "Une librairie, Emilie."

The two girls conferred, expressing delight, while I heard the three boys groan.

"Une librairie très spéciale."

"Pornographie?" one of the boys muttered, and all laughed.

I continued to lead them deep into the Marais, finding my destination with only one error this time. I pointed to the ancient black façade.

"Anglais?" A boy groaned.

I opened the door, and was greeted immediately

by the sight of Lucy's surprised gray eyes. "Monsieur Byrnes...I mean, William."

I motioned for silence, but the damage was done, the two girls had followed me into the store, and began a giggling fit, whispering in an indecipherable patois.

"I have brought some of my students here to purchase some books, Madame Navarre."

She raised her eyebrows dramatically, trying to keep a straight face.

I continued. "Do you have French translations of John Donne, Keats, or Tennyson?"

Lucy's mouth turned into an arch. "Monsieur...I am sorry, but we only have translations to English, not the other way around."

I immediately saw my mistake, and I am sure my face betrayed obvious humiliation.

"But..." Lucy's own face seemed to light up from within. "Perhaps I can help." She began talking very fast in French to the five children. I gathered she was asking what their favorite French books were, and they answered too fast, though I caught one of the boys saying "*Le Grand Meaulnes.*" She bustled them to the hidden staircase, which they clattered down with expressions of alarm.

Lucy returned to the counter, sitting primly on a wooden bar stool, a wool scarf folded over her shoulder. I stood awkwardly, leaning my gangly frame on the counter occasionally. We talked for a few minutes about the weather, my classes, and the recent street cleaner strike. The afternoon light was filtering through the thick window, and it illuminated her pale face, showing me for the first time a star-shaped scar on her throat. I recognized its origin instantly, and wondered.

"It's nice to speak in English again." Lucy smiled. "Perhaps we can meet for lunch some time. After all, two old married folks like us should be able to challenge French notions of propriety."

"Sure," I said, a little taken aback, my stomach beginning to turn. "Here's where you can reach me at the École."

"You haven't mentioned your wife." Lucy tapped my ring finger, shocking me with both her question and her touch.

"She's not…no, I haven't." I said. "No."

Lucy's steely, dagger eyes bored into me, and I felt again that Athena herself was measuring me, finding me lacking.

"So, we can sit in a café, pretend we are experts on Balzac, and not discuss our marriages?" She chuckled.

"Okay." I smiled.

Just then the two girls popped out of the cellar, followed closely by the boys. "Monsieur Byrnes, he try to touch me," one of the girls squealed. I sighed, and a few minutes later led the little monsters back across the length of the fetid, ancient swamp.

*   *   *   *

MEANWHILE, I had begun to explore the markets of Rue Montorgueil more often, starting with the boulangers with their baguettes and loaves of fresh *pain*. I even had a croissant one day before class instead of oatmeal, feeling guilty about the buttery flakiness, and the delicious chocolate that nearly squirted onto my ironed white shirt.

I avoided Cygne, not wanting to be bullied into further decadence. But although I had not hoped for it, a message from Lucy arrived. "10:00 Saturday morning, meet me at the Fontaine des Innocents." But instead of chocolate happiness, I was filled with dread. I had not talked with…anyone…for years now, much less a woman with shoulder-length chestnut hair. What would I say? What if she asked me questions I didn't want to answer? What if she brought up my ring again? I began to panic, going back to my diet of rice and oatmeal for a few days, spending hours unnecessarily preparing for class. But on Saturday morning after oatmeal, I angrily threw on my black wool overcoat and stormed down the Rue Saint Denis to the fountain. I walked around the four-sided Renaissance archway, watching the water cascade down a series of curved steps. But she wasn't there, and I felt a sense of relief, until a clear American voice rang out behind me.

"There you are! I brought us breakfast." She handed me a cup of steaming coffee and a warm croissant. My nemesis. I took them in black gloves and avoided looking at her. "Merci."

"Let's eat and walk. There is no better place to walk than Paris, even in the winter." Her brown hair bounced away toward Les Halles. "And tell me about *The Belly of Paris*. I don't remember it at all, if I even read it."

"If you read it?"

"Well, when you work in a bookstore, it all sort of blends."

"Hmm...well, let me think." We reached the iron pavilions that were left when the markets were torn down and wandered through the park. I told her of lush beds of cabbages, of tanks full of fresh turbots and eels, of butchers smoking and rolling meats into sausages. We walked down Rue Jean Jacques Rousseau, turned onto Saint-Honore, and reached the Comédie-Française while I regaled her with tales of the shopkeepers and market sellers living their greedy little lives. I mentioned how the main character, Florent, is sent back to Devil's Island for being one of the "thin" people.

"Are you one of those?" Lucy poked my arm with a chuckle.

"Maybe." I tried to laugh.

"Well, Monsieur Byrnes...I mean, William," she inflected clearly, making a joke out of our informality. "We may have to work up an appetite today."

We did, walking under the colonnades of the Rue de Rivoli, past expensive stores and tourist traps, while Lucy questioned me about my teaching. I told her the same thing I told Cygne, but Lucy probed further.

"What did American Lit mean to you?" She asked obliquely.

"Uhm...freedom of the individual, I guess. The opportunity to exercise will, you know, the pioneer, the cowboy, the philosopher hobo riding the rails."

"Why switch to the Brits?"

I sighed. "Those railroad myths stopped traveling so well." I said, a prepared answer that I had given a job interviewer once.

"Uh-huh. So, the dissolution of social structures appealed more?" Lucy pointed out the enormous obelisk in the Place de la Concorde before turning us along the Seine, giving me time to think.

"In my opinion, they mostly write about how small errors lead to unhappiness."

"Interesting reading." Lucy stopped on the Pont Alexandre III, peering through the fog. "We can barely see the tower today," she pouted, then marched on towards the golden dome of the Invalides.

I glanced at the shadow of the massive steel lightning rod that helped define Paris. I had barely paid attention to it before now, or any of the city, I realized.

"Hey, let's go see Napoleon," Lucy suggested brightly. "I've never gone in there." She pointed at the Invalides.

"Sure." I shrugged. "Does it cost money?"

She gave me a withering look. "I'll pay for starving teachers today."

"I didn't mean…" I groaned. I was really coming across as a jerk. I reassured myself that Lucy had no interest in me anyway, and just wanted an American sound machine.

We bought tickets and I followed the small woman up the steps of the central building and through security. I began to notice a certain odor, I wouldn't call it a fragrance, that hung around her hair, splashing through the currents of space as she moved. What was it? I couldn't place the scent.

Lucy stopped at the railing and we leaned down at the enormous coffin of Finnish red porphyry. Napoleon's gray coat and distinctive hat were inside glass nearby. Lucy squinted at them. "You know, I think Monsieur Bonaparte would have liked American Literature a lot."

I smiled uneasily. "I think you're right."

We left Invalides, passing the Musée Rodin. Trying to follow her lead, I stopped in front of the glass doors. "Let's go in here. I want to see *The Thinker*."

Instead, I saw the seemingly unflappable goddess flinch, with a look of pain. "No…not today. Besides, I'm getting hungry. Let's go to a famous café. Or have you been to all the literary shrines already?"

"Not one," I said, looking back at the Rodin Museum with a shrug.

"Really…" Lucy's gray eyes slashed into me again, clearly recovered. "You're a strange English teacher, Monsieur Byrnes."

"And you're a strange…actually, what are you, for Keats' sake?" The exclamation slipped out, as it often did, and she noticed.

"I am a purveyor of fine translations, for future reference. And did you say for Keats' sake?" She chuckled in that deep throaty way again

"Yes," I sighed, letting the minutes pass as we walked.

"Well?"

"My father used to say for Pete's sake, and I guess I picked it up. But at some point I asked who is this Pete? And why are we worried about his state of being? So, I changed it to a more appropriate homophone, the poet who died so young."

Lucy's chuckle became a cannonade of barks, going on and on as we walked. "I think I like your sense of humor. It took me a while to find it, though." She stopped and I looked around at the busy intersection of Place St. Germain de Pres. "Take your pick." My new friend pointed at the Brasserie Lipp, the Café de Flore, and Les Deux Magots."

"Les Deux Magots," I said promptly. "It has a weird name."

Lucy's chuckles began again. "You really don't know your French, do you? Magots is treasures."

"I knew that," I claimed, trying to look confident and failing utterly.

"Let's go." She led me inside, tittering. I was greeted by wood paneled walls, sumptuous mirrors, and small plaques indicating the favorite seats of resident writers. We sat by Jean-Paul Sartre.

"He used to come here with Simone Beauvoir and work out his philosophy."

"Oh, this is that place?"

"This and the others…you know Sartre?"

"Sure, a little."

"I thought you were coming to me for a French education? And now I find out you already have one?" She mocked a suspicious glare.

"Monsieur Cygne at the École told me that Sartre and his crowd didn't count."

"Really?" Lucy thought about this. "I don't know, they seem very French to me. What about you?"

"Well, they're not like the other stuff I've been reading?"

"How?"

"The others have passion. Rimbaud, Baudelaire…it's angry, but alive."

"Hmmm…" Lucy stroked an imaginary goatee. "Indeed. I would agree. But I must say that Monsieur Sartre and his crew are very popular with my husband, who of course is very French."

"Yes, well." I said crossly. "I think that I will lump it in with American Literature as bad medicine."

"Medicine? I think the problem with all these books you don't like is that it is easy for people to read them as models for behavior, rather than warnings."

I frowned, having a sudden paranoid fantasy that all these new people in my life were in some sort of conspiracy. So, I changed the subject. "Your very French husband. You must tell me how an American like yourself came to marry him."

"Oh!" Lucy seemed taken aback. "Well, that is a long story, but I'll try to shorten it a bit." She sipped a café crème that had arrived when I wasn't paying attention. One had appeared in front of me, too, and my paranoia resurfaced. Had I been zoning out, or worse, gazing at her pale, pretty face like an idiot?

"When I first came to Paris, well, let's just say I was here for school, but was not going to attend in the spring. Nevertheless, I did not want to go back to America…I mean, who does when in Paris?"

I tried not to shrug, and sipped my own coffee, which was simply miraculous.

"So, money was running out and that's when I met the Navarres."

"Your husband."

"No, his parents. They were affiliated with the school, and took me in, so to speak. They let me a little room above their fabulous English bookstore, and in return I worked the front desk, organized the merchandise, et cetera. Their son helped them, but he was away at school."

I thought something seemed missing from this account, but didn't say anything. Lucy was close-mouthed about her past, it seemed. But who was I to complain?

"The Navarres were so amazing, and I became the daughter they never had, according to them. And they… well, let's just say that my own parents were not the most nurturing, and later, well, I couldn't go back…" She trailed off, her concrete eyes glancing at me over her coffee glass.

I pretended not to notice. "And then you met their son."

"Yes, Paul. He didn't come back to Paris until June, and of course was very handsome, and charming, and French, so…" Lucy chuckled a little, and sipped the crème.

"And you got married?"

Her chuckle became a snort. "Not right away! What kind of girl do you think I am? We dated, as I might have called it in America, and he continued business school. Three years later, we were engaged, and the next summer married at the Navarres' house near Orléans. It was quite lovely, and the Navarres were so wonderful, I almost felt like they were my parents, and that Paul, well." She chuckled again. "My husband doesn't get along with his parents very well."

And with you? I wanted to ask. But instead: "They sound like a gift from Paris to you."

"Yes!" Lucy smiled. "Exactly. And the librairie, well, you've seen it, what do you think?"

"Oh, I think a lifetime spent there might not be long enough," I said, half meaning it.

"You're joking, but it really is special. I can just open any book and lose myself, then another..." Lucy trailed off again. I may have been a fool in those years, but I was no dummy. This woman was just as secretive as Athena herself.

We walked back across *Pont Neuf*, since Lucy said she had to be getting back to the store. "Ma mère, Navarre, I mean, will be getting restless. They come in on weekends, but I should really make them dinner tonight."

"I'd love to meet them some time."

Lucy looked at me inscrutably. "That would be... maybe..." She said, then, "How is your apartment? Rats and roaches?"

I tried to smile. "I don't think so, but it is filled with a collection of West African folk art."

"What? How funny."

"Yes, left there by another teacher, a Monsieur Ngoma, I'm told. But why he left them there is a mystery to me."

"Did you ask?"

"Yes, but they all clammed up when I mentioned it. I could ask Cygne, I guess."

"Very exciting," Lucy gushed. "It's your own private mystery to solve, William!"

No, you are, I thought. "I'm not really the detective type," I said out loud.

"Well." Lucy stuck out her gloved hand and shook mine firmly. "We should do this again some time. But make sure to read more of those books I gave you. I want an honest opinion." With that, she turned and marched down Rue de Rivoli past the Tour de St. Jacques.

*   *   *   *

THE NEXT FEW WEEKS are the fondest in a lifetime of memory, I think. One can never be sure,
of course, and the surrounding events have colored
this time a bright blue. But those next four weekends,
walking Paris with Lucy, finding cafés for a crème and
a chat, will always be precious and precise. During the
week I devoured the books she fed me, finding pleasure
in the cleverly executed stories of Guy de Maupassant,
the comedy of Voltaire, and the romances of Alexandre
Dumas. I returned from the École at three, stopping at
the Rue Montorgueil to buy a wheel of cheese or a fine
sausage, and spent the next six or seven hours reading
until bed. In the mornings I no longer relied on oatmeal,
but stopped for a baguette on the way to work, devour-
ing it slowly throughout my classes. The exception was
Saturday, when I waited at the Fontaine des Innocents
for Lucy to arrive. She always had a croissant and coffee
in her slim hands, walking briskly toward me.

One day we tramped the length of the Canal St.
Martin, crossing and re-crossing it on splendid arched
bridges. We sauntered up and down the Champs-
Élysées, pretending to be rich Americans. Another day
we walked to the Luxembourg Gardens and watched
the bocce players for three hours, while discussing *The*

Count of Monte Cristo and its ripple effect of prison break stories. Though it was winter, the Parisians never seemed to lose a step, and I don't remember ever feeling too cold to walk a few miles more.

There was one day, though, when the wind whipped along the Seine a little too smartly for my taste. Lucy and I were browsing the famous quay booksellers, and she was lamenting the decline in their quality.

"Shouldn't you as a purveyor of fine translations be glad that they are selling this stuff?" I picked up a plastic Eiffel Tower pin, then put it back on a shelf full of novelty Moulin Rouge windmills.

"I suppose." She wrinkled her nose. "But it just doesn't speak well for our city."

I was cold and not really thinking when I noticed the Musée d'Orsay's huge railroad station bulk looming to our left. We were passing the rhinoceros statue, and I turned onto the terrace. "Look! There's always a long line, and no one today. We should check it out." I didn't wait for her answer and strode into building up to the guards, who patted me down roughly. Lucy was not with me, standing at the revolving door uncertainly. Only then I remembered the first experience at Rodin, but it was too late. The guards were waving me through to the ticket counter. I gave my companion an encouraging wave and mouthed, "Come on!"

As I purchased the tickets I heard Lucy's voice. "William," she began. "I'm not really in the mood." But the tickets were in my hand, and we were in front of the gift shop already.

"We don't have to stay long. Let's just warm up for a bit. We can even make fun of the art if you don't like the Impressionists."

"No, that's not it." she snapped. "Don't expect me to have a good time."

I tried to look in her stormcloud eyes, which were down on the floor. "I can't imagine you not having a good time," I blurted out stupidly.

She chuckled, but hollowly, I thought. Nevertheless, I led her into the huge central hall, which was populated by expressive statues and a crowd of doorways to choose from. We tried one and browsed past Corot, Ingres, and Delacroix. Lucy was silent, and I tried to fill the space with banal comments, like "That guy looks mean" or "Check out the dog in the corner of that one." No response, and her porcelain hands clenched tightly around her gloves, a posture I had never seen before.

We wandered across the hall and found works like Monet's wintry white *La Pie* and Manet's lushly sexual *Le déjeuner sur l'herbe*. I was quite stunned by the collection, and it came back to me that I had not entered a museum in five months in Paris. Suddenly, I realized I had lost Lucy. I waited a few minutes in a nexus hallway, but she didn't appear. Maybe she moved ahead, to an upper floor. I took the stairs and found Rodin's sculptures and symbolist paintings. I stopped briefly in front of *The Lamentations of Orpheus* by Alexandre Seon and began to feel nauseous, gagging a little at bad memories. Now I didn't want to be here.

I moved through the rooms at a lightning pace, searching. The bookstore maven was nowhere. I bounded up the escalators to the top floor, where I slowed down, finding the Renoir and Degas soothing, their soft lines and bright living portraits cheering me a little. Then I saw Lucy.

She was sitting in the next room, which was rainbowed with Van Goghs. Her foggy eyes were blank, staring at the self-portrait with its sky-blue shirt and wheatfield hair.

"I saw another one in Amsterdam," I offered, sitting down. "Many years ago. I was too young to appreciate it then. I was more interested in…well, in the hash bars," I lied awkwardly.

Lucy said nothing for a minute, and we just stared at the painting. Van Gogh's haunted eyes bored into mine the same way hers did. Finally, a whisper emerged from deep in her throat. "You shouldn't have brought me here."

"I'm sorry," I said. "But I wish you'd tell me why." My mind whirled through possible reasons, but my suppositions were all absurd.

"I can't…it's stupid. I was a different person back then." She shook her head.

"Just tell me what this painting means to you, then," I urged.

"This one? It's nothing, just Van Gogh's eyes; they're accusing, don't you think?"

I nodded, but for some reason didn't want to let her escape. "Is it this place? Did something happen?"

"It's just a museum, William," she snapped.

I continued pushing, and only Van Gogh knows why. "Lucy, you can tell me. We're friends, aren't we?" I said, not so sure now.

"It has nothing to do with…damn it, why did you bring me here?" Her voice rose as she stood up, then sat down again. A docent moved to the doorway in front of the Degas sculptures where he could watch us.

"I'm sorry I hurt you. If you tell me why…" I broke off this tactic. "Listen, Ms. Doubleday!" Her eyes shot to mine. "I am your friend, and you are going to tell me what is wrong."

"You're not." She stopped and her eyes swept around the room. "This all brings up bad stuff."

"Bad stuff is my bread and butter. That's why I read so much."

Lucy did not laugh as I hoped. But after a moment she continued. "I didn't tell you why I came to France? No, of course not. I came here to study painting at the École des Beaux-Arts. But before, I was in an accident, a car accident. I am…afterwards the doctor told me that my hands, my small motor coordination… Well." She drew in a deep breath as if to control herself.

"You were on life-support." I said, shrewdly and probably cruelly.

"Yes, how…the scar." Her hand went to her throat and she glanced at me with a frightened frown. "They said there was…brain damage." I could see that she was doing everything she could not to cry. "I came that autumn to Paris, and I failed. Or rather they rejected me."

"And that's when the Navarres helped you."

"They are trustees." Lucy shrugged. "And they took pity on my condition." Her hands opened and closed rapidly on her gloves. "So now you know why I've avoided places like this." She looked back at Van Gogh, then at the floor again. Her shoulders were hunched, defeated.

I wanted so badly to fold her into my arms just then. But I didn't. Oh, for Keats' sake, I didn't.

*   *   *   *

THERE CAME A DAY SOON AFTER that when I couldn't avoid Cygne any longer. He came to observe my class, though it seemed he came reluctantly, to fulfill an obligation to a rule.

"I must watch you today, for a report," he grumbled, shoving his huge limbs into one of the tiny chairdesks in the back. The students glanced nervously at this intruder, giving him a wide berth. They all must have had Cygne for class at one time or another, and clearly he was one of those teachers, unlike me, who was given enormous respect.

The subject of the day was Tennyson, and after discussing the language of "The Eagle" and "The Splendor

Falls," lost on their francophone ears, I tackled "Ulysses."
Cygne had been feigning sleep, or actually napping, I
couldn't tell. But now his black eyes snapped open and
he smiled.

"What is Ulysses saying to his crew in this poem?" I
asked in a rote voice.

The students gave me the usual silence, but one of the
boys raised a hand.

"Yes, Jacques."

"He is telling them that they are old." The others
laughed.

"That's right." I attempted a smile. "How does he feel
about his family?"

"He loves them?" One girl snickered. "Duh."

"No, *stupide*, he hates them." Another stuck out her
tongue.

"Well, I wouldn't go that far. But he certainly is looking for an excuse to leave."

At this I saw Cygne's broad mouth turn upside down,
and he looked around at the students, as if waiting for
one to disagree.

I continued. "He's restless, and has, as he says, a
'hungry heart'. In other words, he is unsatisfied, and so

he wants to wander again, as he did in *The Odyssey*, a story that I know you've all read."

A crash made everyone jump. "No, Monsieur Byrnes!" Cygne barked. The desk part of his chair had cracked off. "I am sorry, but I know this poem, and I must disagree."

I was completely taken aback, stuttering and stammering. "Well, there are many...interpretations, and, uh..." I muttered. The students were not looking at me anyway, but at Cygne, who was holding the broken piece of wood in his hand like an axe.

"That may be, but how do you explain that he is..." Cygne grabbed the textbook from a terrified student, and scanned the page. "Looking for a 'work of noble note' and wants to 'seek a newer world.'" The huge man nodded at the students. "He is not wandering, not escaping. He goes to explore, to fight, to be un homme."

I shrugged. "I suppose you could read it that way. We each see what we want to." I looked at him with pleading eyes, trying to stop this interruption.

"No, Monsieur Byrnes. You must see this. Tennyson writes here 'I cannot rest from travel: I will drink life to the lees.' This poem tells us that we must swallow the ocean, Monsieur."

Now I was angry. "But he leaves his wife, after she waited twenty years for him to come home. Not to mention his son. He wants to go back to the 'frolic welcome' of his youth."

"Bah!" Cygne waved the desktop, and students squealed their chairs in all directions. "S'il vous plaît. The tone of the poem itself does not allow such readings. There is no wrongdoing here, only the best of human qualities, the résistance to death, the refusal to surrender. Monsieur Ulysses will not collaborate with his mortality."

"Sure," I said weakly, wanting this to be over. "That's a good reading, Monsieur Cygne. Merci."

The giant lapsed into silence, placing the desktop on the floor. I finished the class by moving quickly to the "Charge of the Light Brigade," a poem I despised, and which I lamely connected to the statements about resistance.

The students filed out, and I heard them explode into conversation in the hall. Cygne stood up, smiling. "Je suis désolé. I should not have interfered with the progress of your lecture."

"That's all right," I said, though I was still fuming.

"No, no. You must let me make it up to you this Saturday evening. I will take you to my favorite restaurant here in the Marais."

"That's not necessary," I protested, wanting anything but a dinner with this loudmouthed oaf.

"I insist. You will meet me at the corner of Rue Etienne-Marcel and Montorgueil at twenty hundred hours."

"I really don't…"

"Come, Monsieur Byrnes. We must, as Tennyson tells us, 'drink life to the lees.'" He winked at me and strode out, looking back. "That is…an order?"

I never hated him more than at that moment.

*   *   *   *

L UCY AND I HAD NOT MADE PLANS for that Saturday, and I wasn't sure that she even wanted to see me again. But I was at the Fountain of the Innocents anyway, thumbing through the poems of André Breton. I had lost myself in the verse, and only realized how late it was when I saw the cafés opening for lunch. She wasn't coming and I had run out of books. Should I head to the Rose? Or perhaps somewhere else entirely, I thought bitterly.

As I was deciding what to do, I heard my name. It was Lucy, standing awkwardly in the shadow of the fountain, and she was not alone. A younger man with long black hair tied loosely in a ponytail stood next to her, with a cigarette dangling from his mouth.

"Bonjour, Monsieur Byrnes," Lucy said. "This is Paul."

I stood up and extended my hand. "Bonjour, Monsieur."

He took it limply. "Bonjour."

Lucy indicated the canvas bag at her side. "I brought you more books. I've told Paul about our little literary lunches."

"Yes." I was confused by this whole scene. Was this a friend of hers? A regular customer at the shop? Surely not…

"Oui, Monsieur. When I discovered that mon epouse had a new friend, I told myself I must have to meet you."

I reeled momentarily. This man was five years younger than Lucy at least, and though his features looked all right to me, he wasn't the fine Merovingian nobleman I had pictured.

"Perhaps somewhere close by?" Lucy said, and I heard desperation in her voice.

"Bien. I know a place." I turned and led the couple across Les Halles, my mind in turmoil. I stopped in front of Au Pied du Cochon, right at the base of Saint Eustache Cathedral.

"Oui, I know this place!" The young man, who I thought of as Navarre, cried. "This is for tourists."

"Is it?" I asked. "Perhaps another café then?"

"No, no." Navarre smiled. "I love these places. They are, how you say, kitsch."

"Right." A smartly dressed waiter led us to a table by the windows, which looked out onto the bare winter garden, and the curve of the Bourse de Commerce. Paul began talking very quickly to the waiter in French.

"I have ordered for us," he announced.

That was the beginning of one of the worst meals of my life. I picked at the food, which looked appetizing enough, and so did Lucy. Navarre wolfed down soup and bread, cheese and pâté de foie gras, while plying me with questions about books I had read, always ending with, "Oh, well. If you had read such and such, you would know…"

Lucy said very little, only answering Paul's more obscure inquires, when I floundered. However, when Navarre paused, taking a huge bite of bread slathered with duck liver, Lucy broke in, addressing me almost like we were friends.

"Monsieur Byrnes, I have found your Nigerian teacher."

"Really?" I leaned forward with interest. "Where?"

She chuckled. "I misspoke, I guess. Apparently the mystery is bigger than we thought. He disappeared."

"Well, I know that."

"No, I mean he really disappeared. There was a manhunt by the police, and a bit of a scandal for the École. That's why no one talks about it."

"Scandal? How is it their fault?"

"He was about to be fired for something, and the police investigated. All very hush-hush."

"Did they ever uncover anything?"

"No. The most popular theories in the papers were that he got in trouble with a French girl, and either had to leave, or was killed because of it."

"Killed!"

"Well, it was only a theory. I think it is much more likely he fled. Besides, it could have been something else entirely. No one ever found out."

"Wow."

"Maybe there are clues at the apartment?"

"I don't think so, but maybe I should dig around a bit."

Navarre had been watching this exchange with cold blue eyes. "So, Monsieur, how is it you have come to us here? Does your wife not miss you?"

A shock ran up my arm. "She's…"

"Don't bother him about that," pleaded Lucy.

"Well, I just find it interesting. I am curious about the domestic relations of others."

Lucy looked out the window, flushed.

I cleared my throat. "She's not…I mean, she's gone."

"Oh ho!" Navarre reached across and slapped me on the shoulder. "I am sorry, mon ami. There are so many getting le divorce these days."

"Well…" I began, then closed my mouth. Let him think what he wants to. I glanced at Lucy, and saw her slate eyes drilling into me, and looked away, flagging down the waiter for l'addition.

Navarre kept it up. "I notice, however, that you wear your ring. This is unusual."

Infuriated, I turned on him, not thinking about Lucy. "I notice that neither of you wear yours. This is unusual, too. No?"

"Ah, that is because I do not let her! Here in France, marriage is…society? It is for the purposes of taxes. She is no slave to wear a manacle." Navarre laughed, draining his glass and letting me take the check.

I looked at Lucy and saw she was blushing fiercely, and caught a flash of rage before she looked down into her lap. During the meal, I had caught wafts of that puzzling scent emanating from her brown hair. But now I recognized the smell, and snorted at my stupidity. It was the stench of books.

Outside, we all shook hands like strangers who had just met, and Lucy offered me the canvas bag silently. I walked north, past the Cathedral, across Etienne-Marcel, and up Tiquetonne. At the apartment I found that the pencil I often kept in my pocket had been snapped into six pieces. I felt a great revulsion welling in me for Navarre, for Paris, and for myself. There were five hours until I had to meet Cygne, and I collapsed on the small couch, ready to leave France on the next plane rather than do so. Nothing mattered anymore, and this cursed city had become my hell.

*   *   *   *

WHEN I ARRIVED AT THE DESIGNATED SPOT, I saw Cygne poking around in a Lebanese market across the street, inspecting the forty-odd baskets of grains and lentils. The fresh greens and rich yellows of these varieties of rice, wheat, and beans dominated the front of the store. I joined him, and he pointed at the red lentils. "Those are of the highest quality. Make sure you come here for your dry goods." I nodded absently, still full of ire at his treatment of me earlier that week.

Cygne pointed across the street to what appeared to be a giant golden snail presiding over an ornate black façade. Gold lettering proclaimed "L'Escargot Montorgueil." Cygne noted my skeptical eyebrows. "You will love it."

I slouched behind him as we brushed past the encased menu and white umbrellas, and through the heavy front doors. An immaculately dressed man immediately took our coats, while another greeted Cygne. The interior breathed through dark wood, mirrored with plush red seats and crisp white tables lit by gold sconces of candles. The maître-d' escorted us to a table in the back, moving it to help my companion slide his enormous body behind it. Before we had a chance to look at the menu, a somme-lier popped out of a red curtain, greeted us, and had an argument over wine with Cygne too fast for me to catch. Other than the swallow with Cygne a month earlier, I hadn't tasted alcohol for years. But I was ready that night, hoping it would bring sweet oblivion.

I looked at the menu, finding numerous escargot appetizers, as might be expected. Frog's legs, quail, foie gras, urchin, veal kidneys, turbot, l'angoustines, mullet, duck…I hadn't tried anything on this list. I shrugged. Why not? I was going to get the most expensive, strangest stuff I could find tonight. "Would you like to share the thirty-six Burgundy snails?" I asked my torturer.

He looked at me with surprise that changed to a smile. "Oui, Monsieur Byrnes. In a Chablis cream sauce?"

I nodded. "I'm ready for anything."

"Bien! I think you will enjoy this wine. It is one of my very favorites."

I shrugged, looking around at the other patrons, finding that I was slightly underdressed, even in a tie and pressed white shirt. There was one man in the corner in a sweater and jeans, but he looked familiar, and I was nearly sure he was a movie star.

Cygne followed my gaze and nodded. "Yes, this place attracts many celebrities. In the past, Salvador Dali, Sarah Bernhardt, and of course my favorite author, Marcel Proust. You have not read Proust yet?"

"Not yet."

"Save him for last." Cygne smacked his lips.

A waiter took our order for the escargot, and another announced the specials in French, then in English for me.

"I'll take that, the roast goose with charred foie gras."

"Bien, Monsieur." The waiter seemed taken aback by

my American abruptness.

Cygne ordered "les langoustine de Loctudy" just as the wine came. It was dark and red, a beautiful Burgundy Grand Cru from Cote de Beaune. Cygne tasted it, approved, and then offered a toast when my glass was poured.

"Monsieur Byrnes, I am afraid that I have been rather rough on you. Here is to a poor memory of what a bastard I am."

I smiled a little, taking a sip. Notes of caramel and cherry were laid over a rich center of loamy chocolate. I breathed in, and the aroma fused to my membranes, making me dizzy. Cygne watched with approval. Sure, I hated this man, but he knew how to pick a wine.

"I haven't had a fine wine for many years now. In fact, I haven't drunk anything." I admitted, not caring what he thought of me anymore.

Cygne shrugged. "Well, Monsieur, there is always time to start again." He didn't press further, and perhaps because of that, or perhaps the wine, when the thirty-six escargot arrived in a luscious cream sauce, I no longer felt angry. We used the snail tongs and fork, pulling enormous gastropods out of blood-striped shells, and they were tasty, tender, not rubbery or tough at all.

"These are just what I needed," I said, realizing how hungry I was. "I had an awful lunch."

Cygne grunted, spearing a snail. "Why is that?"

"Oh…it was with a woman."

"What is the problem, then?"

"Her husband was also there," I pronounced bitterly.

"Ah…" Cygne finished his half of the snails, and sat back into the plush cushions. "You are involved in *un tragedie*. I should have known?"

"No, it's not a tragedy," I protested. "I mean, this part isn't. But she was in an accident, and her husband is a lout, and Van Gogh scares her…" I realized I was babbling, and popped the last appetizer into my mouth to shut up.

Cygne did not laugh, and instead inspected my face closely. "Be careful, mon ami. All love stories are tragedies, it only depends how far into the future you go."

I drank the burgundy, which tasted even richer now that it had aerated a bit. "I wouldn't know."

Cygne motioned to the waiter, and he poured us more wine. "Van Gogh knew, mon ami. Perhaps that is why he scares you."

"I said he scares her."

"Ah, well, our painter friend could teach you much. I suggest you visit him."

"He's not French, he's Dutch." I pointed out. "Not part of the curriculum."

"But his soul was not of the Low Countries. He wrote in French, he lived in France, he died in France. We must claim him as our own!" He slapped the table, causing the hovering waiters to hover more uncertainly. Then he looked at me slyly. "Be careful, Monsieur Byrnes, or one day we may claim you, too."

"Now I really am scared."

My companion did laugh at this, and slapped the red cushions. "Come, mon ami, tell me instead about your reading. I assume you have read beyond *The Belly*, no?"

"Oui." I considered. "Many more, in fact."

"Mervielleux! What are you reading right at this moment?"

I thought back to Lucy's canvas bag, which I had opened a few hours earlier, with Rousseau, Valery, the Goncourts, and on the bottom, as if hidden, Flaubert. "Well, just before I came tonight, I started *Madame Bovary*."

"Mais oui. But if you just started, let me not ruin it for you. Instead, tell me what is your favorite so far?"

And so, we talked through the savory dinner, ordering desserts of brandy-soaked pastry that made me even drunker than I already was. Cygne ordered coffee, and it was midnight before I shook hands with this paradoxical Frenchman, generous and abrasive, friend and enemy. Stumbling home along Tiquetonne, I noticed for the first time a fondue brasserie directly adjacent to my apartment building. What was wrong with me?

*   *   *   *

ON MONDAY ANOTHER NOTE ARRIVED in my box at the École, longer this time, in Lucy's exquisite handwriting.

"Dear William. I am so sorry for what happened to our day. Paul was home this weekend, and after a huge argument, he insisted on meeting you. I'm sorry I didn't tell you more about him before, but as you witnessed, he can be quite jealous. I was so hoping you would have left already, and then I could have explained everything to you later. Most weekends he is not in Paris, even though his business classes are during the week. He has what my parents in Massachusetts would call a 'rich social life.' This must seem like a small problem to you, having gone through a divorce. But you can see why your friendship has meant so much to me these past weeks. I hope you can forgive me, and I would like to try again this Saturday. If you can bear it, please come by the *Rose* Saturday morning at our usual time. Lucy"

Of course I went. I wasn't a complete jerk. I bought coffee and croissants and showed up at her little bookstore fifteen minutes early. The door was locked, and I waited outside, until Lucy popped into the street.

"Isn't the store open today?" I asked.

"Ma mère will do that soon." Lucy took the coffee and bit heartily into the croissant. "We'll go east today, if you don't mind."

"Sounds good," I said, smiling.

Lucy smiled back. "Thanks for coming, by the way."

We wound out of the Marais labyrinth and through the Place de la Bastille, discussing the merits and defects of the enormous glass and steel opera house. Then we turned up the Rue de la Roquette, where Lucy detoured into a flower shop. "We have to make a quick stop." She purchased a small bouquet, and we continued along the avenue, talking about our shared ignorance of European architecture. She told me about visiting the Navarres' country house near Orléans for the first time. "It's not exactly a mansion, but it's big enough to house a large family and their goats. The first time I went, Paul's grandparents were still alive. They were so sweet to me and spent that year of weekends teaching me old French recipes."

"I've been trying a few of those myself," I said. "But I haven't had an authentic instructor to help me along."

"Well, maybe…" Lucy stopped herself. "Anyway, they died shortly after that, and their funeral was when the Navarres formally invited me to be part of their family."

"How's that?"

"Well, it wasn't maybe as formal as you're thinking. But they offered me a place at their table every night, and turned one of the rooms at the house into a permanent space for me."

I hadn't been paying attention to where we were walking, and as Lucy turned through an open gate, I looked up and saw a hill of crypts unlike anything I had ever seen before. It was an actual city of the dead, with cobbled avenues lines with elaborate tombs. A wave of anxiety flooded my esophagus.

"Uhm, where…" I muttered.

"Père Lachaise, of course. I've just been telling you. It's their anniversary, and I wanted to stop and say hello." She held up the flowers.

I couldn't very well say no, and so I followed her through the rows of mausoleums. She pointed out

Heloise and Abelard's shared tomb, and listed all the authors buried here. "You really ought to see some of them, since you've been reading their books."

I nodded, slowly getting used to the place. I mean, it wasn't really like a cemetery at all, more like a collection of monuments. Almost like a museum, except for the ravens filling the air with croaks. I saw one dragging a small piece of wood, and wondered if it was from a coffin.

"They're just up here." Lucy pointed out a steep rise. Was there no end to this labyrinth of death? I focused on my black boots as they navigated the uneven paths and staircases. At the top of the hill, Lucy turned right to an area of tightly packed tomb walls. My shoulder brushed against a particularly mossy slab. A raven flew overhead with what I was sure was a bony finger in its mouth.

Lucy stopped at a mid-size tomb with "Navarre" lettered over the rusted metal door. Inside was a small shelf and a partially broken stained glass window. She laid the flowers on the shelf. "Hello, grand-mère. Hello, grand-père. It's been another year, and I just wanted to let you know that things are great. I'm making new friends, and really getting to know your city even better. I hope you'd be proud of me."

That was sweet, I thought, that she included me. And this wasn't so bad. It bore no resemblance to the other cemetery at all.

Lucy smiled, and we threaded our way out of the maze, and along an avenue transversale. "I think Balzac is right around here," she said.

"All right," I muttered.

"Are you okay?" Lucy stopped and turned to me with concern in her granite orbs. "You look terrible."

"I'm fine," I lied. "Maybe I need some food."

"Sure. Let's see Balzac first. We can come back after and see Proust and all the rest."

I nodded, trying to keep my eyes on the ground. Suddenly, I heard crying. Glancing up, I saw an older couple kneeling by a tomb, arranging pots of flowers. Their faces were streaked with grief.

I had to get out. I turned and began walking fast, not caring if Lucy was following, feeling my legs turn to rubber. A moveable green trash bin had been placed on the avenue, and, yanking it open, I was sick.

I was finally able to step away and sit down, staring at my boots. Lucy sat next to me.

"You should have mentioned you were ill."

I shook my head mutely.

"No…it's this place, isn't it?" She asked sharply. "Come on, let me help you."

I accepted her arm, though I didn't deserve it, and hated myself more. We limped down the hill and out a corner gate. Near the metro station was a café called Le Saint Amour. Lucy led me inside. "Deux, s'il vous plaît." She added something else, and the waitress took us to the corner behind a pillar by the window. I looked at the brown paper that covered the small table, aching for calm.

"Thé, s'il vous plaît. Et pain." I heard Lucy tell someone. Then: "William, I'm sorry." Her voice was coming to me through a long tunnel. "Did somebody…did you lose someone?"

"Lose," I said. "That's funny."

Lucy ignored this. "Was it…oh my goodness, I'm so stupid. Was it your wife?"

"She's not…" I shook my head. "Lucy, stop it."

"Oh, William," she said, and folded her hands in her lap. Minutes passed, and the tea and bread arrived. My stomach had settled, and I picked at the handfuls of baguette. Lucy sipped her tea, and though she was obviously trying not to, her eyes periodically flicked toward me like spotlights.

"I want you to tell me, William," she said softly. "Please."

"Tell you what? That she was not my wife, just my fiancée? That's she's dead. That I have never been back to her grave since the day she…since her parents…" I tore a piece of baguette in half. "Is that nice? Do you sympathize with me now? Am I a tragic fellow?"

Lucy said nothing, her eyes steady and penetrating.

"Do you really want to know, Ms. Doubleday, or Navarre, or whoever you are? I doubt it, but I'm going to tell you anyway," I hissed. "Maybe then you'll leave me alone."

I saw the pain I caused with that remark, but pressed on. "Yes, I had a fiancée and she loved me. But I was young, and stupid, and full of my sense of personal freedom. So…she found out, I guess, about the other girls… and I came home to a note and this ring, which she had bought me and was saving for a surprise." I tried to take a sip of tea, and nearly choked. "So, real romantic, eh? That's what everyone thought, like I was some Orpheus mourning Eurydice. Because I never showed anyone that note, and never told anyone this story."

Lucy was silent for a minute. "What was her name?"

"What?" I realized I had not ventured that particular detail. "Ann Marie."

"How did she...do it?"

"The garage. Carbon monoxide. I found her," I said listlessly.

"That must have been terrible," Lucy said, and I still heard sympathy in her voice.

"Don't you get it? I never loved her. I killed her. I am not a nice person."

Lucy sipped her tea, looking out the window. "Was she nice?"

"Nice? What does that have to do with it?"

"I don't know..." Lucy sighed. "It's a very disturbing story, William. And you should take responsibility for your actions. Is that what you'd like to hear?" She tried to chuckle, but it came out as a cough. "But she didn't have to do that. We are each responsible for our lives."

"Comforting," I said bitterly.

"Hey!" Lucy snorted. "Don't take this out on me."

"Oh...I know. You're so good it makes me a little sick."

"Good?" Lucy realized she was raising her voice, and dropped it again. "I was...the accident? I caused that. The boy driving, well, I had a certain reputation, and we had been drinking…" She speared me with those eyes. "I was encouraging him, you know, to drive fast. And I was… not in my seat, and we crashed."

Now it was my turn to be shocked. "Did he…"

"No, he was almost completely unhurt. But it quickly got around how I had caused the whole thing, and with my reputation as the town…well, that was also the last straw for my parents. They refused to come to the hospital, I'm told."

"How could they?"

"I had been the worst daughter that a pair of strict Puritan folk could imagine. I couldn't blame them."

"I could."

"This from the man who only blames himself."

"You didn't hurt anyone else."

"Didn't I? I wonder." She paused, sipping the tea. "And hurting yourself might be the worst sin of all."

I frowned, puzzled.

She continued, "Anyway, we apparently have a lot more in common than you think."

I tried not to let myself get pulled into this trap, but couldn't help it. "Really? How much do you hate yourself?"

Her eyes registered shock, then she recovered. "At

least you admit to that much. But that's not it, really. I'm just…I'm a different person. We have many lives, and this is mine right now."

Later, I wondered at the import of those words, but at the time, well, I was in no condition. We finished the tea and she led me back along the Rue de la Roquette toward the Opera Bastille.

"You are a little like Orpheus." She poked me in the arm. "Or rather you think you are, torturing yourself. Don't you see, you haven't really changed. Orpheus was self-centered right until the end."

I nearly stopped walking in shock. "How…" I couldn't believe she was saying this, after her comforting if misguided words in the café. How was I being selfish? A few blocks after the Bastille she turned off with a wave. At that moment, I wished I had never met her.

*   *   *   *

ON THE WAY TO AUVERS-SUR-OISE, I exited the train at the wrong station. I have to say it was not entirely my fault; the exit had the same name on the sign as the next one. But once done, I had to wait for the next train coming out of Paris a half-hour later. I gnashed my teeth and tried not to curse Cygne for recommending this trip. Of course, it was my own fault. I never would have braved the Ile-de-France RER system if I wasn't avoiding something.

Finally, after a lonely, rainy time at that station, and the next, and a tense moment when through inattention I almost missed my final stop, I walked from the small, deserted station into the empty town. I found the village map and slouched my way down the main street to the Auberge Ravoux, which was transformed into the "Maison du Van Gogh." The metal gates were padlocked and the charming tavern, which Cygne had assured me "served authentic French food" was dark. I cursed and thought of other ways I could be spending the day. Reading Montaigne's Essais, or walking the Tulieries with her...

I wandered up the narrow side street to the Musée Daubigny, which was also closed. The tourist office was open, though, and they cheerfully offered me the chance to buy postcards of scenes that Van Gogh painted of the town and surrounding area. I declined and stomped down the concrete stairs, past an old rick converted to picnic area, and up the long hill in a pouring rain. The Église Notre Dame Auvers appeared at the top of another staircase. It was covered with wet, olive moss and abandoned scaffolding. I hunched inside, shaking off my black wool coat. The transept was empty, and a small old woman praying in the nave was the only sound. I sat down in one of the wobbly wooden chairs, throwing my coat over another.

What was I doing here? Why did I think this would be an escape? Nothing I did let me off the hook, no matter what Lucy said. I did not deserve her sympathy, her advice, or her friendship. And the idea that I could be happy, an idea that had secretly bloomed in me these last weeks, fed on literature and art, on food and cama-raderie? Well, that was the most selfish idea of all. My mind ran on like this, and I sat there for nearly an hour, long after the old woman had hobbled out into the rain. Slowly, my brain cleared, emptying of all memory, all analysis, all questioning. Only the hum of the church's heating system mattered.

The bells tolled fifteen hundred hours. I walked out, prepared to leave Auvers-sur-Oise, but as I opened the door, a splash of sunlight brushed in. I looked back, and the stained glass was glowing like a basket of fruit. How had I not noticed? Now, I had no excuse, really, not to follow the signs, past the fallow winter wheat fields, past the murder of crows that picked through the muddy earth. At the top of another long hill was a cemetery, surrounded by a pitted stone wall. Inside it was an enormous square, full of ordinary graves instead of magnificent vaults. Strangely, it didn't bother me as much this time. Only a few twinges of fear ran through my stomach as I walked around the edge of the burying ground to his grave. Or rather, two graves, because I had forgotten that his brother broke down only a few months after Vincent perished. Someone had placed plastic sunflowers by the tombstones, and I could see that behind them along the wall, real ones waited patiently for spring. Small trinkets and postcards lay buried in the bed of ivy that grew over both graves like a warm blanket. I pulled one out of the dirt. The writing was Korean, a language even more indecipherable to me than French.

People all over the world connected with Van Gogh. Why? His painting, of course. But it wasn't just that. There were many painters, even at his level of excellence. No, it was also his story, I supposed. It contained all the things that made literature interesting: insanity, genius, tragedy, failure, but also friendship, integrity, loyalty, heroism… People connected with the story, because it was their own. People connected…

As I stood there on that upland of the crows, alone on a winter day with the two brothers, my mind followed two tracks. The first was the simple one: that I must absolutely convince Lucy to paint, that it was my duty to encourage her as Theo encouraged Vincent, that the only way that sunflowers grow is if someone plants them. Such effort was probably futile, and most likely would have the opposite effect. But that didn't matter.

The second was of another grave, one that I had never returned to. That was my duty, too. I needed to ask forgiveness, and maybe to say goodbye. It might have been obvious to everyone else, and obvious to me now, but at the time, well, it was a bit of a shock. Lucy's words leaving Le Saint Amour came back to me, and sunk in. I must stop selfishly playing my melancholy lyre, and letting the Furies tear me apart. These two metaphors, brothers, soaked into my body, came together, apart, and together again, until I realized they were the same thought.

"I may not deserve happiness," I said to the silent Van Goghs. "But she does."

At the moss-grown church, a cloud of pigeons wheeled from the tower, dipped toward me, and then flew back to their perches. I detoured inside and dropped Ann Marie's platinum ring into the donation box. A few other

pilgrims passed me on the way up the hill, looking hope-
ful. On the way to the station, I passed the Otto Zadkine
sculpture of Auvers' beloved artist. He looked gaunt and
harried, but faced directly at the fading winter sun.

*   *   *   *

TWO DAYS LATER, I stopped by the Rose after class.
Lucy was sitting at the front counter. "Catch," I said,
and tossed her a furry ball. Startled, she grabbed it out
of the air.

"For your cats." I smiled. "And nice catch, by the way."

"Thank you," Lucy said primly, inspecting the toy.
"The cats say thank you."

I continued my assault. "I mean, I've seen you shelve
those books, too. You could be a professional juggler."

"Ha, ha." Lucy tossed the toy back at me. I missed
it, and one of the cats sprang out of nowhere, batting it
between the stacks.

"Guess I need to work on my hand-eye coordination."

Lucy said nothing, eyeing me suspiciously.

"Listen, I wanted to apologize for what I said after the
cemetery. I had no right to attack you."

"No, you didn't." She considered. "But it must be difficult for you."

"There you go again, taking my side. I was an emperor-sized jerk."

Lucy blushed, something I had never seen. "Yes... okay. You were. But..."

"But," I interrupted. "That's over now. Can we be friends again?"

She smiled, and then I heard that throaty chuckle. "Monsieur Byrnes, you never cease to surprise me."

"Well, the reason I'm here is not a surprise. I'm looking for a book."

"You've come to the right place."

"Could you find me the second volume of the Goncourt Brothers' journals? I find them hilarious."

"I know right where that is. Back in a jiff."

While she disappeared downstairs, I rifled through the papers behind the counter. There was a "to-do" list Lucy had written out that was checked off. I pocketed it. She brought the book upstairs, I paid for it, and gave her a cheery goodbye.

On Thursday afternoon I returned. When I poked my head inside, she wasn't there. Downstairs, then? No, after a quick circuit of the cramped but strangely comforting area, I only found a tortoiseshell cat wrapped around the catnip toy I had brought. I petted her and creaked back up the stairs, just as Lucy was emerging from a door behind the counter, which with my usual denseness I had never noticed.

"Whoops!" We said at the same time, both startled at the entrance of the other. She chuckled, and I smiled.

"Hello, Ms. Doubleday. I have something for you today, and I need you to promise not to be mad."

"What's that?"

"Promise?"

"Absolutely not." She chuckled again. "You've got a bad reputation with me now, pal." But then, perhaps thinking how this could be misinterpreted, said, "But I promise to pretend not to be mad. How's that?"

I considered. "Very well." Laying the folder I was carrying down on the counter, I tried to smile brightly, actually terrified at how this could all backfire on me. Luckily, the black cat jumped onto the counter, apparently thinking I had brought another toy. Lucy stroked the cat, and opened the folder. It contained the "to-do" sheet I had stolen from her earlier that week, and a signed letter, which was in very formal French.

"You'll have to translate, I'm afraid." I knew the gist

of what it contained, but wanted her to get it from the letter, not from me.

"This says." She held up the letter. "William, what…"

"Just read it. And since I couldn't read most of it, maybe you'd better tell me."

"It is a letter from a Monsieur Haineau. It states some credentials…"

"Haineau teaches at the École, but he's also a professional handwriting expert of some sort. I think he works for the government. Read the second paragraph."

"It says something like, this handwriting sample comes from a woman with excellent hand muscle skills. It is my professional opinion that she has no damage to her nerves. It also has some scientific information, and then says…oh, William, why?"

"I've seen you do things, and I didn't think you knew."

"Knew what?"

"What the letter says…that any damage you sustained has been healed."

Lucy was almost crying. "I can't believe…"

"I'm sorry, but it's the truth. I had to tell Haineau a little about you, but I didn't tell him about the accident until after he examined the writing. He said he would have never known."

"I don't…"

"He said that often steady work with the hands can completely heal the sort of damage you sustained. Something about restructuring neural pathways." I waved at the bookstore. "You've been in rehab all this time, and you didn't even know." I petted the black cat. "And I'm sure the demanding petting schedule helped, too."

Lucy nodded, choking a laugh out. "You really are a jerk, you know."

"I know," I said, smiling. But I decided that was enough for that day, leaving with a friendly wave. Let it sink in. When I returned to the apartment at Rue Tiquetonne, I hung the Louis Armstrong picture back up on the wall. What had I ever had against it?

$$* \qquad * \qquad * \qquad *$$

ON SATURDAY WE MET at the Fontaine des Innocents without either of us mentioning it. She had two café crèmes and croissants, which, to my surprise, were filled with ham and cheese instead of chocolate.

"I'm hungry today," she explained.

"Excellent. Well, we can eat them on the metro," I said, leading her toward the Les Halles station.

"What, are you sick of walking?" She chuckled, mouth full of pastry.

"We'll walk back. But I'd like to go somewhere this morning before it gets too crowded."

"How mysterious," Lucy mumbled.

"Careful there, don't choke." I smiled, and led her to the Porte d'Orléans platform. The train pulled up seconds later, and we boarded, sitting down on the folding seats and finishing breakfast. At the Montparnasse Bienvenue stop, I lunged out like a sprinter, and Lucy followed, snorting and chuckling.

"Sorry…my last experience on the trains was not so good." I led her through the passage and up the stairs to daylight.

She blinked as I led her up the hill toward the skyscraper. "Are we going up the tower? I must warn you that Paul took me up there for a date." She laughed.

I cringed, but shook my head. "No, not at all."

At the Boulevard Edgar-Quinet, I turned her to the left, and she saw where I was taking her. Her feet slowed, and before she could say anything, I smiled. "We're going to the cemetery," I lied. "Don't panic."

"Oh, okay," she said, and followed me into the marché de la creation, an outdoor art market forming an alley in the wide central island of the street. The sun was out, and the green awnings had been rolled back. A few artists were still setting up their paintings and objets d'art, placing them on folding tables and hanging them on wires that led along the cloth panels which separated the stalls.

"Maybe you can help me out here," I said in an offhand way. "I can't tell which of these artists are good, and which are just dabblers."

"Well, I think they're all good. I'm sure they have to apply to display here."

"Right, but there's obviously a range of quality. Like this one here." I pointed to a stall full of landscapes. "Are these any good?"

Lucy shrugged. "Well…"

"Be honest." I wagged a finger.

"They are not very good," she whispered. "I don't know if he understands English, though."

"Ha…well, let's talk about each one at the next stall, then?"

We moved to the next pair of booths. "Okay, well, he seemed like he was trying too hard to make his paintings look like Monet."

"Was he?"

"Yes, maybe. But he's just copying someone else's style. He's not an artist, he's an impersonator."

I nodded. "What about these two?" We inspected both stalls and moved to the next.

"The woman on the right is making very nice little pottery, even though it is obviously geared toward the tourist trade rather than display in a museum. The man on the right is just splashing paint on the canvas."

I smiled broadly at this. "That seems like a lot of modern art to me."

"No!" Lucy protested, then recanted. "Well, okay, much of it is that. But some of it may look like that, but to a trained eye, it is pure genius."

"Pure genius, eh?" I nodded sagely. "Well, let's continue."

We walked slowly down the rows of artists, past line drawings, handmade jewelry, and cartoons, playing critic. Near the end, almost at the walls of Cimetière Montparnasse, Lucy stopped in front of a stall full of portraits. They seemed little different than some of the others to me, but she had a rapt expression on her face.

"Bonjour, madame," the gray-bearded artist said, sipping a coffee.

"Bonjour, monsieur. Votre art est très bon."

"Merci!" The old man seemed quite pleased. They began chatting in French, and I faded into the background, pretending to scrutinize a stall of cat paintings. As the minutes wore on, I walked quickly back along the row to where I had seen something inexpensive to purchase. When I returned, Lucy was shaking the man's hand and taking a business card. "Au revoir."

"Au revoir, madame."

We continued browsing, and once we had gone a sufficient distance, I asked, "Well, please tell me why his art was so much better than the others."

"Oh!" Lucy seemed surprised. "Isn't it obvious?"

"Not to me." I shrugged. "I'm a barbarian, remember."

She laughed. "Well, the lines, the colors, the strokes of his brush, the way the faces burst from the canvas. It's inspiring. Look at this one." She pointed to another painter's canvas. "The weakness of the lines, the uncertain tones. In the other, well, the spirit given to us through color and light...quite extraordinary."

I nodded and smiled. "By the way, while you were chatting with le artiste, I got you a present."

"No! William, you shouldn't have..." She peered into the bag, and pulled out a children's art set, complete with tiny pastels, brushes, and watercolor cakes.

"I figured you could start small." I grinned, praying to Van Gogh that she would take it the right way.

Mercifully, she dissolved in snorts and chuckles. "You are a barbarian."

We walked to La Rotonde for lunch. Lucy ordered a goat cheese, prune, and apricot pastry with salad, and I got a tower of leeks with beet sauce and a hard-boiled egg on top. We talked for three hours straight without stopping, during which I noticed that she either didn't remember or didn't mention that I had said we were going to the cemetery.

"Thank you for today's lecture, Ms. Doubleday," I said, as we tramped down the long hill of the Boulevard St. Michel.

"Now it is my turn to remind you to call me Lucy," she returned softly, her hand brushing against my glove lightly.

I spent that entire night lying awake in the tiny bedroom, listening to traffic on Rue de Turbigo. I deserved it, I tried to tell myself. I deserved every torture in the book.

*   *   *   *

I WASN'T ABLE TO GET OUT OF THE ÉCOLE that week before seven due to midterm examinations. The teachers seemed restless, and the administrative work I had let pile up needed to be done. So, I arrived at the Rose on Saturday, early, feeling like I had not been there in a year. Lucy greeted me cheerily. "How were the little monsters this week?"

"The usual. Do you have the French lesson book you mentioned last time?"

"Upstairs somewhere." Lucy stood up and opened the door behind the counter. "Come on up while I find it."

"Okay…" I followed her up the narrow, turning staircase. At the top, another door opened into the apartment, which I reminded myself Lucy shared with Navarre. It was furnished with an eclectic mix of art deco and Swedish thrift, and I realized I had been expecting some sort of Second Empire hôtel. I could see Lucy inspecting one of at least ten jammed bookcases with a frown.

On the table was a sketchbook, not the kiddy one I had bought her, but a real one. It was unfortunately closed, but a used charcoal pencil lay on top. I began to smile, and then I saw the cradle. It was leaning against the wall by the front windows, half in the sunlight, but at first I didn't realize what it might mean.

"I've got it," Lucy said, beaming triumphantly. "Come on."

I turned and edged down the steep stairs, feeling her following. As I emerged into the warm belly of the Librairie, I began to think terrible thoughts. But then, as I stopped to pet the black tabby, I felt Lucy's slim hand on my shoulder and those thoughts fled.

"Let's take a walk along the river," Lucy suggested. I nodded and we wandered down to the Pont de Sully, where we crossed the Ile Saint-Louis, and ducked down to the wide quais. The massive stone walls with their ancient iron rings seemed to enclose us in a private world. A woman passed us, walking a dog, and an old man and his grandson tottered ahead of us, until we overtook them near Notre Dame. The cobbles were wet with recent rain, and a few times I caught Lucy's arm as she began to slip. She smiled, and continued regaling me with a tale of her childhood in Massachusetts, walking the Freedom Trail in Boston. When she was finished, I told her about exploring Philadelphia with a school group, and my college graduation dinner at the City Tavern, drinking George Washington's beer. As we crossed the Seine at the pedestrian Pont des Arts, heading towards the Louvre, I actually stopped and spun around, taking in the grandeur of the city.

Lucy watched me with an inscrutable grin, her gray eyes twinkling merrily in the slanting winter sun. "Is it home yet?"

"Maybe." I laughed.

She led me down to the quai again, past an accordionist playing a melancholy tune, and we ducked through the tunnel under Pont de Carousel. An enormous sycamore branched out into the river. Lucy pointed to the huge clock of the Orsay across the river. "It seems like a year ago that you knocked the wind out of me there."

"Well, you paid me back at the cemetery."

She laughed, putting the French lesson book down on the cobbles. The sycamore had an extensive root system that made it seem as if the tree was melting into the stone. Lucy stood on it and touched the mottled bark. "They look gray from a distance, but up close…"

I moved next to her and put my hand on the bark near hers, surprising her.

"You're really very tall," Lucy muttered, looking away, then back up at me. I could smell the book smell again, and it made me lean toward her a little. Suddenly, she stood on her toes and those gray swords plunged into my eyes.

One second, maybe two, and I pulled back. "Wait…"
I said, remembering the cradle, and maybe the grave.
"We can't…"

Lucy stepped back in surprise. "If you knew…what it
meant…" She bit her lip, seeing something in my face that
I swear wasn't there. And then she was gone, vanished
up the stone staircase. I hurried after her, but she disappeared into the huge crowds headed for the Louvre,
leaving me standing there on the edge of the Tulieries,
feeling like I had felt when I first met her, a fool. She had
just risked everything: the parents she never had, the
Librairie Anglais Rose, even Paris itself. And I had turned
her down, out of some noble principle that I couldn't
even name.

*   *   *   *

THE NEXT DAY, WHILE MOROSELY frying up onions,
a diced sausage, and green beans, I began flipping
through Monsieur Ngoma's collection of books. They
were absolutely jammed with notes, in French, of course.
But then, leafing idly through some book on colonial-
ism, I found a small yellowed flower pressed between
the pages. I remembered Lucy's idea about clues, and

hypothesized maybe the police hadn't been thinking like a history teacher. There must have been three or four hundred books, but I had time. Maybe I would learn a few words of French by osmosis while I was at it.

I had gone through maybe a hundred books when I found a postcard. On the front was a photograph of an elephant, faded with age. The postmark was only a year old, however, and though the writing was in French, I was able to puzzle it out as I finished my lunch.

"Everyone is well at home, dear brother. Since mother and father passed, it has been difficult, Lord knows. But we have persevered. We do worry about the troubles you mentioned in the last letter, and hope that God will help you do his will. I miss you and pray we will be reunited soon. There is so little time to any of us. Love, Rachel."

So little time. I had made a terrible mistake, an epic mistake, worthy of the most terrible villains in literature. I had to tell her. I flew down the streets, getting lost again near the Picasso Museum and popping through the front door of the Rose as if storming the Bastille. At the counter was Navarre.

"Bonjour, Monsieur Byrnes!" he exclaimed, pushing his long, black hair from his face. "Comment allez-vous?"

"Bien...I was looking for Madame..." I trailed off.

"Oh? Why is that? Are you perhaps sleeping with her? I hope not, for then I would have to kill you!"

I sputtered, but then saw his boyish grin.

"No, I am joking. I know that mon epouse would not do such a thing." He lit a cigarette, tossing the match casually behind him. I cringed, glancing at the books, and he continued. "However, I am sorry, but Luce is not here. How do you say...pay-rents? They have taken her to our little house in Orléans for a few semaines."

I sagged, knocking a book off a shelf. I picked it up, and noticed the title: *Fathers and Sons* by Turgenev. "Is it because she is pregnant?"

"Pregnant? What do you mean?"

I thought a minute. "Enceinte."

At this, Navarre laughed, tapping ash onto the counter. "No! My Luce is, as you say, sterile. She did not tell you of her accident? Yes, I have married a woman who will not bear me children, and I enjoy it that way."

"But the cradle..." I said weakly, without realizing it.

"The cradle? For her beloved *chats*?" He looked sharply at me. "Then you have been sleeping with her, upstairs in the bed we share. That is really too much." He stood up uncertainly, obviously thinking he needed to do something about this intolerable situation, but was not sure what.

"No," I said coldly, finding my strength. "We went upstairs to get a book. A book, you little…" I realized my gloves were clenched tightly around the Turgenev. The young man sat down again, looking at me with surprise. "A book, Monsieur Navarre. Only a book." I pushed out the door into the March breeze, my long legs striding down the narrow streets unconsciously, until I reached the Place des Vosges and I collapsed on a park bench, shaking with rage and regret.

The houses squared around me like the walls of a monastery. Children played on a giant sandbox that sunk into the ground amongst the sycamores. A band of violinists and cellists was warming up underneath the colonnades near Victor Hugo's house, and I listened to Vivaldi, then Mozart, then something else I had never heard, a rousing folk song that echoed off the brick facades, reaching a terrible crescendo that left the scattered onlookers clapping and hooting.

I thought of the disappeared Monsieur Ngoma, and wondered how he had managed such a marvelous feat.

*   *   *   *

THE NEXT DAY I WAS AT THE FACULTY MAILBOX, thinking perhaps she had left a note, when Cygne called me into the tiny lunchroom. He was popping black olives into his mouth, but without the usual zeal.

"So, as you have no doubt heard, I will no longer be teaching here, Monsieur Byrnes."

I sat down, dazed. "No."

"No? Yes. But perhaps you do not know? You are not French. I have been fired, as you might say, for an indiscretion."

Indiscretion? I decided not to ask, but Cygne answered.

"Yes, an indiscretion that has been the downfall of many a heroic teacher, if you take my meaning."

I did, and I hoped she had been one of the seniors, at least. "I'm sorry to hear that, Monsieur."

He continued his combination of self-pity and glorification. "Yes, it has been the downfall of many a French hero!"

I thought of Madame Bovary, and others. "And many a French heroine, as well."

"Oui, oui," he said impatiently. "And so, Monsieur Byrnes, you are ready now for an examination? Mais oui. What is the key to French Literature?"

I sat back in the small chair, thinking of Alain-Fournier's *Le Grand Meaulnes*, which I had just finished reading. "Well, I don't like to generalize."

"But as a teacher, you must," he prompted.

"From my limited exposure, I would say it is about the inevitability of loss."

Cygne did not answer for a minute, spitting seeds into the trash bin.

"Okay?" I asked, trying to grin.

Cygne swallowed an olive. "Yes, *okay*, Monsieur Byrnes. I will accept that answer. Tout perdus." He heaved his mighty frame up, slapping the table. "And I must tell you that the teachers of this school will not take my firing on the ground. They plan to strike."

"Strike?"

"Oui. They will have fraternité with the heroic Cygne in his fight against the repressive regime of École Eustache."

"When?"

"Soon, soon. I am afraid that will mean you will be on holiday for a bit, Monsieur. Perhaps longer. Perhaps you will spend some time with the charming mistress of the

Rose that you have told me so much about."

I had told him nothing beyond our discussion at L'Escargot, and reeled in surprise at both his insight and the freshness of the wound. "No…I don't think I will see her again."

Cygne put on his overcoat. "No? Then perhaps you understand French Literature more than I. Or soon you will." He moved his broad frame through the door, leaving the open jar of olives on the small table.

He meant that parting shot as one of his many exaggerations, of course. But the mysterious implication became clear later that week, when I received notice that my contract would not be renewed. I went to see the woman who had hired me, and she gave me a sympathetic clucking with her tongue.

"There will be a strike, you see? So all contract teachers are to be let go. There will be a final check, but unless you have the means to stay in Paris until autumn, when I may be able to help you again…"

"Not really."

She seemed relieved to hear that. "It is for the best. There is no guarantee of future work."

"So, the faculty support for Monsieur Cygne put me out of a job."

"Monsieur Cygne?" She laughed a little, then remembered why I was there. "No, it is for greater pay that the teachers strike, you see. It is also beautiful weather in April, and many of them want to be home, out of the city."

Now it was my turn to laugh, if bitterly. What a hero. But then, as I walked down the long hall, a wave of relief and foreboding flooded my thin frame. Now I had no choice but to leave Paris, and return to Philadelphia, to the tasks that awaited me there. It also meant giving up hope of ever seeing Lucy Doubleday again.

*   *   *   *

I HAD A WEEK TO PUT THINGS IN ORDER and vacate the apartment on Rue Tiquetonne. Suddenly, every avenue I had walked took on meaning and value. The boulangeries and boucheries on the Rue Montorgueil began to smell even fresher. I made a circuit of all the nearby cafés, blowing breezily through my small savings, savoring every morsel of cheese and every sip of café crème. I visited the Louvre for the first time, strolling the endless halls and galleries until the boots began to crush my feet. I also wrote five letters, but couldn't seem to get the words right, and they went into a drawer at the apartment, to be found by the next owner, I supposed.

On my last day I rambled down to Notre Dame and sat in the transept again, though this time instead of a pleasant thoughtlessness, it brought a stone balustrade of memory crashing upon me. Choking, I hurried out, rushing unthinkingly to the Seine. I was at the corner of the little park I had avoided, the one that stretched below the south windows. And there beside me were the purple flowers that reminded me of Ann Marie's grave. But now that empty memory was full, and I felt the terrible strength it had taken to fill myself. Of what? I didn't know, but I knew that tomorrow I would have to take one more walk around this city that had become, so briefly, my home. After that I would pack for the airport, making sure to steal my predecessor's photograph of Louis Armstrong. And as I thought that, the pigeons swept in around me, and it was all I could do not to laugh.

Checking my box one last time at the École, I found *Le Petit Prince* by Antoine de Saint-Exupery, with a note: "From my personal bibliothèque—Cygne." I shook my head. Who was I to judge him? We were two brothers if any were. And he had given me so much, the least of which was French Literature. I would send him an American book when I returned to Philadelphia. Perhaps *Leaves of Grass* or *On the Road*. There was some strong stuff in those about travel and goodbye.

*   *   *   **

MANY YEARS LATER, as they say in so many of those books that fill my rooms, I spied the name Doubleday in *The New York Times*. I often did, here and there, it being a common enough name. But it was in the Arts section, and I paused, scanning the page. There was "Lucy," as part of a group of Parisian painters showing in a small gallery in the East Village. Without thinking, really, I got in my car, braved the New Jersey Turnpike, crossed the George Washington Bridge, then headed down the east side to the exit by 25th street. I parked in a garage near Union Square and walked past The Strand bookstore to where the address in the *Times* said the showing was. It was a strange building for an art gallery, I thought, looking up at the facade of an old bank. The door was open, and I walked inside. A very young woman in black tights and turtleneck sat at a desk.

"Is this the Paris showing?" I asked, and for a second expected her to say "Oui."

"Yes, sir. Please leave your name and information here."

I jumped through the hoops, and without looking up asked. "How many pieces by Ms. Doubleday are showing?"

"Just one, but...well, you'll see."

I frowned. "Is the artist in the city?"

"Yes, in fact she may be in later today."

I walked through another door, as if to flee that information, still half-wondering at this strange venue. And then I saw why. A canvas splashed across an entire wall of the former bank, at least thirty feet long and fifteen high. It was a helicopter view of the Marais, from the Left Bank to Gare del Est and from the Opera Bastille to the Louvre. But it was colored in a summer I had never imagined, bright and rich, with intricate detail beyond my weak impressionistic imagination. There was Les Halles as it once had been, bustling with lively markets. Half-inch high figures strolled the avenues, past the high crowns of churches and into crowded squares. Individual trees marked the length of the streets, theaters exploded with actors, and the river swarmed with boats.

I was staggered. It was art as a goddess might have imagined it, if she had the soul of a librarian. I found the Rose after a minute, and there she was, the artist, her brown hair and dark Victorian dress hemmed between a pair of sycamores. My first thought was regret that I was not rich enough to buy it, or even house this majestic monstrosity, this arrondisement with a thousand tiny stories for me to read and discover anew.

I moved back and forth in front of the painting for an hour, finding a tiny Picasso outside his museum, and a red-haired man I thought might be Van Gogh heading up the Rue Sebastopol. And then…I stopped. Near a Saint Eustache that towered above Les Halles, I saw a small sign that read École. Beneath it was a half-inch high figure, one among the thousands, thin, with a long, black coat, walking east. I began to shake, then, telling myself that I was too old for such nonsense, I wiped tears that refused to stop.

"Would you like to leave a message for Ms. Doubleday?" The young girl at the desk asked as I was putting on my coat.

"No…yes." I hesitated.

"She will be here soon, sir. Perhaps you would like to wait?"

I considered for what must have been two full minutes, while the girl looked at me with a bemused expression. Then I scribbled a note: "Beautiful. Thank you." I left it unsigned and walked to the open expanse of Union Square, finding a seat on a bench underneath the elms. Children played nearby, shouting with simple delight. The statue of Lafayette watched me out of the corner of his eye. I struggled with my decision, and I couldn't help expecting to hear her ringing voice, to find her bringing me croissants and coffee. But of course she didn't, and I left the square to browse the crowded shelves of The Strand.

There were plenty of books inside that would help me welcome the ever-changing splendor of life. They would likely tell me: *it's better that way, William, left as a painting*. They might say: *you are a different person now*. Or maybe not. Maybe they would send me home in ruins. One thing I was sure they would tell me was *remember*. Because the person you become springs from that one shining afternoon, somewhere in the future past, when you walk out your door and there are rough, cobbled streets that coil past open-air cafes, then splash onto wide avenues twinkling prosily on forever, beyond the golden palaces and granite churches into evening, and suddenly you are on the banks of the Seine, the tower crackles with fire, and it's *Paris*, for Keats' sake, and you are not dead, not even dying, and something opens inside you, something fine, and true, and light.

ABOUT THE AUTHOR

Eric D. Lehman teaches literature and creative writing at the University of Bridgeport and his essays, reviews, poems, and stories have been published in dozens of journals and magazines. He is the author of eight history books, including *Homegrown Terror: Benedict Arnold and the Burning of New London*, and *Becoming Tom Thumb: Charles Stratton, P.T. Barnum, and the Dawn of American Celebrity*, which won the Henry Russell Hitchcock Award from the Victorian Society of America and was chosen as one of the American Library Association's outstanding university press books of the year. He is also the author of the bestselling travel guide *Insiders' Guide to Connecticut*, the Pushcart-nominated memoir *Afoot in Connecticut: Journeys in Natural History*, and the short story collection, *The Foundation of Summer*.

CPSIA information can be obtained at www.ICGtesting.com
Printed in the USA
BVOW08s1549120716

455210BV00002B/2/P